W9-BIV-832

GREAT BIG GRIZZLIES

By Ryan Nagelhout

 Gareth Stevens
Publishing

Please visit our website, www.garethstevens.com. For a free color catalog of all our high-quality books, call toll free 1-800-542-2595 or fax 1-877-542-2596.

Library of Congress Cataloging-in-Publication Data

Nagelhout, Ryan.
Great big grizzlies / by Ryan Nagelhout.
  p. cm. — (Great big animals)
Includes index.
ISBN 978-1-4339-9433-3 (pbk.)
ISBN 978-1-4339-9434-0 (6-Pack)
ISBN 978-1-4339-9432-6 (library binding)
1. Grizzly bear—Juvenile literature. 2. Bears—Juvenile literature. I. Nagelhout, Ryan. II. Title.
QL737.C27 N34 2013
599.784—dc23

First Edition

Published in 2014 by
Gareth Stevens Publishing
111 East 14th Street, Suite 349
New York, NY 10003

Editor: Ryan Nagelhout
Designer: Sarah Liddell

Photo credits: Cover, p. 1 Richard Seeley/Shutterstock.com; p. 5 James Hager/Robert Harding World Imagery/Getty Images; p. 7 Jeff R Clow/Flickr/Getty Images; p. 9 oksana perkins/Shutterstock.com; p. 11 Design Pics/Richard Wear/Getty Images; p. 13 Nagel Photography/Shutterstock.com; p. 15 Danita Delimont/Gallo Images/Getty Images; p. 17 Kelly Funk/All Canada Photos/Getty Images; p. 19 (den) S.J. Krasemann/Peter Arnold/Getty Images; p. 19 (bear) Jeff Banke/Shutterstock.com; p. 21 Lindsay Dean/Shutterstock.com; p. 23 Design Pics/Deb Garside/Getty Images.

Printed in the United States of America

CPSIA compliance information: Batch #CS13GS: For further information contact Gareth Stevens, New York, New York at 1-800-542-2595.

Contents

Grizzly bears are huge!

They are a kind
of brown bear.

They eat lots of fish.

Some live up to 25 years.

They weigh up to
800 pounds!

They can stand up
on their back legs.

Some can grow
8 feet long!

17

They dig a hole
to live in.
This is called a den.

19

They stay there
when it gets cold.
This is called
hibernation.

They have babies
in the winter.

23

Words to Know

den

fish

legs

Index